Cézanne and the Apple Boy

LAURENCE ANHOLT

BARRON'S

PAUL was playing with his friends
when his mother brought him a letter,

"Look!" she said. "It's from your father!"

Paul had not seen his father in a long time.
He knew that his father was an artist who lived far away in the countryside. And Paul had exactly the same name as his father. It was written on all of his school books:

Paul Cézanne

Paul read the letter...

Then something fell out of the envelope.

It was a train ticket.

His mother packed some food in a little bag.

She put him on the train and kissed him good-bye.

It was a long journey and the motion of the train put Paul to sleep.

When he woke up, he saw a mountain.

Paul walked out of the station and into the little town. At last he found his father's house, but there was no one at home.

"I'll tell you where you'll find him," said a lady. "Halfway up the mountain, painting crazy pictures!"

So Paul stepped onto the winding path which led out of town and into the mountains. It was very hot and the path was steep.

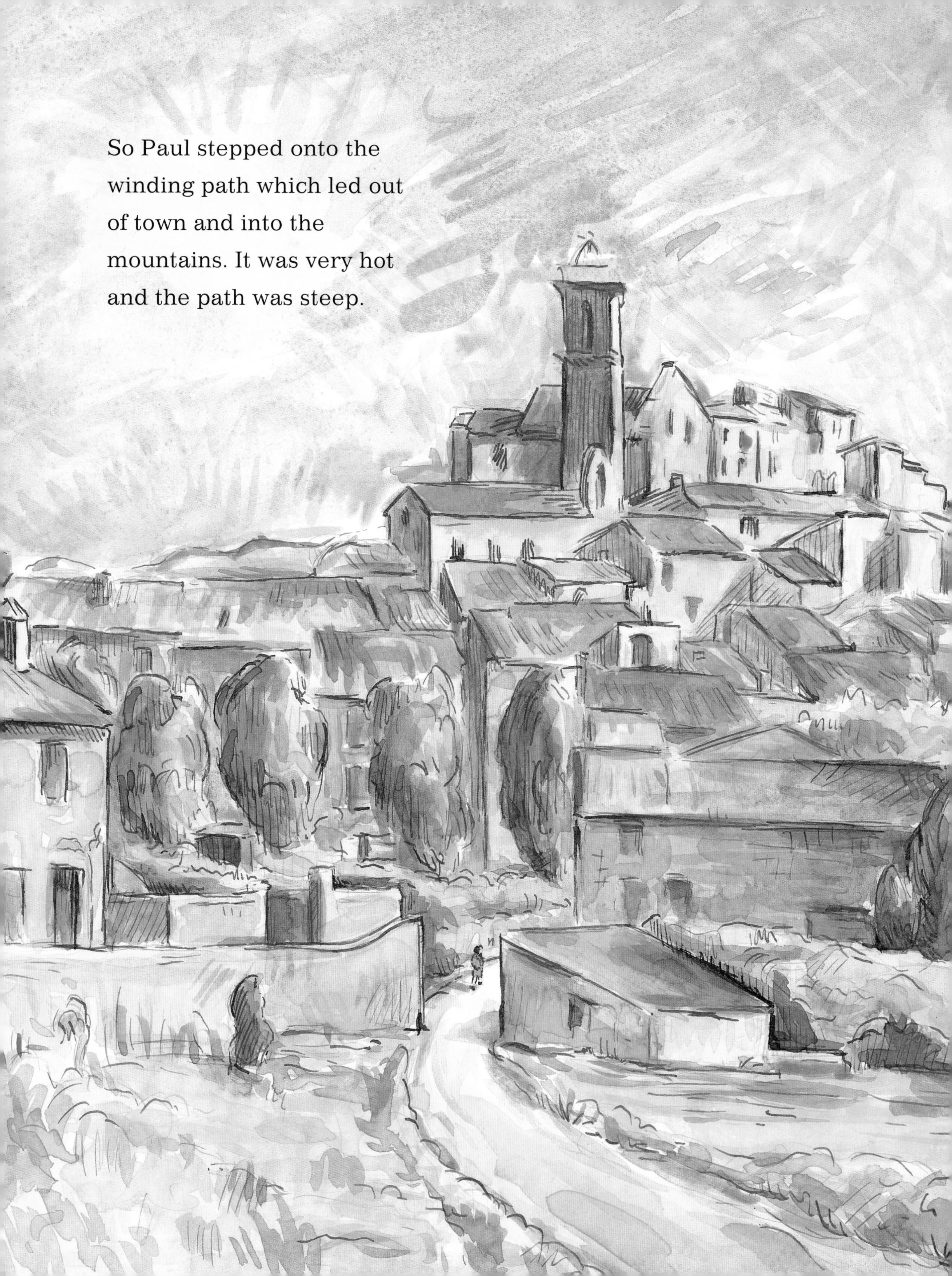

In the shade of a tree, a donkey was munching apples.

Someone was talking to himself nearby.

Paul peeped around the corner.

"OH!" he shouted.

High on a rocky path
he saw a man as big as a bear.
He was making a wild
painting. He had a shaggy
beard and wild eyes.

Paul ran back down the path.

“Paul, Paul! Don’t you remember?
I am Paul Cézanne – the same as you!
I am your father.”

Cézanne was as big as the mountain
but he spoke gently.
“I am very pleased to see you,” he said.
“But I will not shake your hand...
You see, I do not like anyone touching me.”

Then the mountain man packed up his paints,
and set off along the path.

"We are going on a journey right to the top of
the blue mountain," said Cézanne. "It's a long way,
but if we follow the path, we won't get lost."

“We haven’t got much money,
but look, we have plenty of apples…
and plenty of paints and canvasses.”

“You look after the donkey.
And I’ll look after you.”

When it grew dark,
they built a fire by a little stream.

"Tomorrow I will paint a picture of you,"
said Cézanne. "But you will have to sit
as still as an apple."

Then they fell asleep
under the stars.

When Paul woke up, Cézanne was sorting his paintings.

"You see, Paul," he said, "I am inventing a new kind of painting...

"I make everything into simple shapes. I paint houses like boxes; and trees like cones. Everything has a shape."

"What shape am I?" asked Paul.

"You are as round as a sweet little apple!"

They followed the winding path through
a valley and into a dusty village.

The people in the café stared at Cézanne and laughed at his pictures.

“What have you painted today?” they snorted. “A crooked house or a wobbly tree?”

“You see, Paul,” his father sighed, “the world doesn’t understand me and I don’t understand the world. That’s why I spend my time in the mountains…”

“…And that’s why you are so poor, Mountain Man!” laughed the people in the café. Cézanne stood up and walked toward the door.

“Just a moment,” said a voice behind them. “May I see that picture?”

Paul turned around.

A man with a bow tie and an expensive suit was staring at his painting.

"This is extraordinary," he said. "I would like to take this picture back to my art gallery in the city."

"My name is Vollard. I am an art dealer and I am always looking for exciting new work..."

"Well, we have more paintings than we can carry," said Cézanne. "Take as many as you like... Have this one ... and this one!"

So Vollard left with a huge pile of paintings.

Paul ran after him. "Please, Mr. Vollard," he whispered. "Look after these paintings. I think they are very special. I think my father has invented a new kind of painting."

Then Paul helped his father pack up his paints. As they walked out of the dusty village, they could hear the people laughing.

"Ah, Paul," said Cézanne, "sometimes life is as hard as climbing a mountain."

"The people are right, my paintings are worth nothing at all."

At last there was no money left.
"I should find a job," said Cézanne.
"The trouble is I am only good at one thing – that is painting."

"I know something else you are good at," said Paul quietly.
"You are good at being a father."

In the distance Paul saw a tiny man, waving his arms and shouting. When he came closer, Paul could see the man was dressed in an expensive suit with a bow tie – it was Vollard!

"Quick, Paul," he panted, "where is your father?"

"My father is working," said Paul. "If you want to buy a painting, you will have to talk to me."

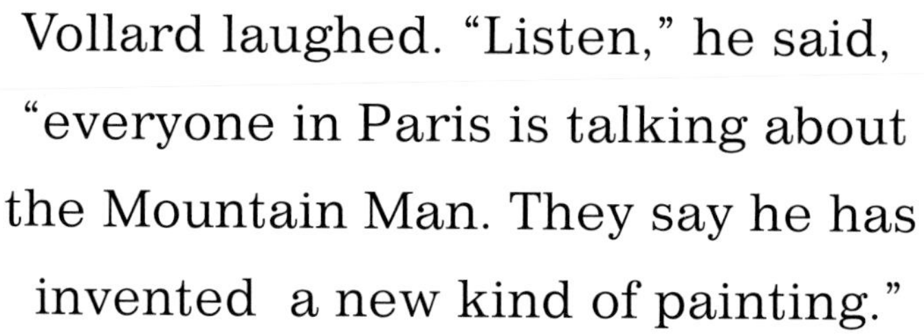

Vollard laughed. "Listen," he said, "everyone in Paris is talking about the Mountain Man. They say he has invented a new kind of painting."

"Of course," said Paul. "My father is the greatest painter in the world."

“What’s all this noise?” asked Cézanne, coming around the corner.

“I’m trying to explain,” said Vollard, “I have sold every one of your paintings! All this money is for you! I want to buy more – as many as you can paint!”

Cézanne stuffed the money in his pocket.

“Thank you very much, Mr. Vollard. I would like to shake your hand … but you see, I don’t like anybody touching me.”

“Now if you will excuse me, Paul and I have to leave. We are nearly at the top of our mountain.”

"Sometimes life is hard,"
said Cézanne.
"But you follow your path..."

*"...AND
AT LAST
YOU REACH
THE TOP!"*
shouted Paul.

Then Paul and his father walked back down the mountain. When they reached the dusty village, Paul was afraid that the people would laugh. But he held himself high.

"I am the son of the Mountain Man," he whispered.

The summer was ending
and the apple trees were
golden-brown. At last
they reached the little town.
And there was Cézanne's
house near the station.

Paul ran so fast he almost
knocked over his mother
who was waiting to take him home.

"Oh Paul!" she said, "I hardly recognized you. You have grown so tall."

"Well, Paul," said his father, "we had a good expedition. I would like
to shake your hand, but...

but..."

"...But I will give you
a big kiss instead!"
said Paul.

When Paul got back
to the city, he ran outside
to see his friends.

He didn't notice,
but something
fell from his pocket –

a tiny apple seed.

Ten years passed. Paul looked outside where the tiny seed had grown into an apple tree which blossomed in the spring. He thought of his father, Paul Cézanne, following his path, high on the blue mountain.

He had became a successful art dealer like Vollard. He sold his father's paintings all over the world and people paid millions of dollars for the paintings of mountains, crooked houses, and piles of apples on wobbly tables.